A dazzling beam of light filled the largest window of the fairy house great room.

"Squeak!" said Squeak.

The light was so bright and powerful that it seemed to be knocking right on the window-pane.

Clara took Rosy's hand and squeezed it tight. "She's come back, Rosy," whispered Clara. "She's come back at last."

THE
fairy bell
SISTERS

Christmas
Fairy Magic

Margaret McNamara

ILLUSTRATIONS BY CATHARINE COLLINGRIDGE

BALZER + BRAY

An Imprint of HarperCollins Publishers

In the spirit of J. M. Barrie, who created Peter Pan
and Tinker Bell, the author has donated a portion of
the proceeds from the sale of this book to the
Great Ormond Street Hospital.

Balzer + Bray is an imprint of HarperCollins Publishers.

Christmas Fairy Magic
Text copyright © 2014 by Margaret McNamara
Illustrations copyright © 2014 by Catharine Collingridge
Map copyright © Julia Denos
All rights reserved. Printed in the United States of America.
No part of this book may be used or reproduced in any manner whatsoever without written permission except in the case of brief quotations embodied in critical articles and reviews. For information address HarperCollins Children's Books, a division of HarperCollins Publishers, 195 Broadway, New York, NY 10007.
www.harpercollinschildrens.com

Library of Congress Control Number: 2014942343

ISBN 978-0-06-226723-8 (pbk.)
ISBN 978-0-06-226724-5 (trade bdg.)

Typography by Erin Fitzsimmons
14 15 16 17 18   CG/OPM   10 9 8 7 6 5 4 3 2
❖
First Edition

for
Becky,
who is the very spirit
of Christmas

THE fairy bell SISTERS

one

"This Christmas will be the perfect Christmas," said Goldie Bell one sparkling December morning. "I'll have so many presents!"

The Fairy Bell sisters were lying on the hearth rug before a roaring fire in the great room of their fairy house. It was a blindingly sun-filled morning, with fresh snow sparkling on every rooftop of the fairy village.

"Only ten more days till Christmas," said Sylva Bell. She was stroking a tiny kitten that was curled up in the crook of her arm. "We

don't know if we can wait any longer than that, do we, Ginger?" she said. Ginger purred.

"Well, you won't have to," said Clara. "Christmas is coming whether we'll be ready or not."

"I'm ready now," said Goldie.

"We'll be patient, won't we, Squeakie?" said Rosy Bell.

"O-bee!" said Squeak.

"Why not, Squeak? Why won't you be patient?" said Rosy. Squeak rolled over and rubbed her back on her crib. "I don't know what's the matter with Squeak. She hasn't been at all herself lately."

"Maybe she's getting a new tooth," said Sylva.

"Or she has an upset tummy," said Clara. "Goldie, have you been giving Squeak fairy chocolates again?"

"Not too many," said Goldie.

"I'm a little worried about her," said Rosy. "Do you think—"

Just then there was a tinkling of bells outside their fairy house windows. "What's that?" asked Clara. The bells had a tone that she recognized from long ago, but she did not want to risk saying what she thought. She flew over to open the door—and found no one there.

"Try the back door," said Goldie. "Maybe it's Avery. She said she'd come visit later on today."

The tinkling sound came again. Rosy looked at Clara. *Could it be?*

Sylva flew to the back door and opened it. "No one here, either," she said.

Once more the bell tinkled. Ginger scurried into the kitchen to hide. "Look! There at the window!" cried Rosy.

A dazzling beam of light filled the largest window of the fairy house great room.

"Squeak!" said Squeak.

The light was so bright and powerful that it seemed to be knocking right on the window-pane.

Clara took Rosy's hand and squeezed it tight. "She's come back, Rosy," whispered Clara. "She's come back at last."

two

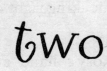

It would be terribly rude to go much further in this story without introducing all of you to the Fairy Bell sisters. If you haven't had the pleasure of their acquaintance already, please meet them now. Here are:

Clara Bell   Rosy Bell

Golden Bell

Sylva Bell

and baby
Squeak

Clara, Rosy, Goldie, Sylva, and Squeak live together with the other young fairies on Sheep-skerry Island, which is a place so filled with magic that you may be reading this story very near it right now (only you might not know it, because human people call it by another name). The Fairy Bell sisters have one more member of their family, their big sister, who lives in Neverland with a friend called Peter Pan. In case you don't dare guess her name, I'll tell you: it's Tinker Bell. And it was Tinker Bell who had made that tinkling sound right outside the Fairy Bell sisters' fairy house.

If you have read other stories about the Fairy Bell sisters, you know that now is the time I usually ask a question to see if you *really* want to read any further. The question could be about perfect fairies or foolish fairies or headstrong fairies or fairies with tender hearts.

In times past, most of you have turned the pages and read on, which is why you know so much about the Fairy Bell sisters. But this time, I'm going to take a chance. I'm *not* going to ask that question, because I believe that every single one of you will want to read a story about a magical little baby who's about to make a big change. A little baby who has a secret language all her own. A little baby named Euphemia Bell, better known as Squeak.

You might especially want to read this story if I add that it is absolutely filled with magic, and it's about a Christmas that almost does not happen—a Christmas that is an absolute disaster . . . until Squeakie Bell discovers the most extraordinary Christmas present in all of Fairyland.

So get yourself cozy, and wrap up warm if it's cold outside. And then let's see if you do go ahead and turn that page. . . .

three

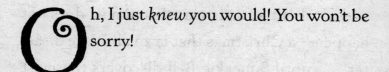

Oh, I just *knew* you would! You won't be sorry!

four

"What is all this?" said Rosy. "Did Christmas come early?" asked Sylva.

Clara pushed open the window against the snow. The beam of light grew brighter and the bell sound was even higher and more clear. The great room was bathed in a brilliant light, which dissolved into a constellation of tiny crystals. The crystals gathered in front of the roaring fire. They didn't melt like snowflakes; instead, they swirled together in midair.

"What is it?" asked Sylva. She had never

seen such a thing before in her life.

But Goldie had. She remembered a message like this on her ninth birthday, a very special message indeed. "It's from Tinker Bell!" she cried.

The moment Goldie Bell said the words "Tinker Bell," the crystals swirled into shapes. And the shapes turned into words. And the words chimed. *From Tinker Bell*, they said.

"Tink!" cried Clara. "Is that really you?"

Of course it's me, the words rang. *Only Tinker Bell can do things like this!*

"It's not Tink herself," Rosy whispered. "But it's Tink's magic!"

"Let's listen to what she's saying," said Goldie. "Quick! Before the crystals disappear!"

The words sparkled and glowed as they chimed aloud.

Christmas is only ten days away, they said. *I know you are working hard to make it the best Christmas ever. . . .*

"We are!" cried Sylva.

But now I want you to stop working and not do another thing. Because I will do everything for you this Christmas.

"Does that mean you'll come home, Tink?" asked Sylva.

"Hush, Sylva," said Clara. "It's magic." The words continued to appear.

I want to treat you to the very best Christmas you could ever have, they said. *I'll bring every single present from Neverland, and a tree too—with special decorations from Peter and the Lost Boys.*

"Ahhma!" said Squeak.

Mind you don't lift a finger. Leave it all to me. I'm in charge this year. See you early on the morning of December 24, if not before! Love, Tink.

The Fairy Bell sisters watched the words *Love, Tink* till they faded from sight.

Sylva was the first to speak. "Do you really think—"

But her words were interrupted by another flash.

PS. I will be very cross if you spoil my surprise by decorating for Christmas and making presents for one another, so PLEASE DO NOT. That means you too, Rosy. xoxo T.

Just to be on the safe side, the sisters didn't speak for quite a long time.

"Do you think she means it?" asked Clara at last. Clara knew from experience that sometimes Tinker Bell had trouble keeping her promises.

"Oh, she'll come! She'll come for sure. And she'll bring Christmas with her!" said Sylva. Sylva had been so young when Tink left for Neverland that she barely remembered her oldest sister. Sometimes she even forgot what Tink looked like. "I want to see her so much."

"Squeakie, aren't you happy?" asked Rosy. But Squeakie, usually the cheeriest baby on Sheepskerry Island (or anywhere else), only gave a tiny smile.

"Squeakie's too young to know much about Christmas," said Goldie, giving her baby sister a cuddle. "But oh my! I can only imagine what Tink will bring me from Neverland. She knows I have exquisite taste."

Sylva was so thrilled that she flew around

the great room in circles at the thought of Tinker Bell being here on Sheepskerry Island. "Now I really can't wait till Christmas," she said. "It's going to be the best Christmas of my entire life!"

five

There's nowhere quite so beautiful as Sheepskerry Island after a snowfall. The land is silent. The trees are laden down with heavy white powder that sparkles with tiny prisms of color. Fairies have wings, of course, but they all love to make the first tracks in new-fallen snow. And that's exactly what the Fairy Bell sisters were hoping to do one week before Christmas.

"The snow's stopped. Can we go outside, Clara?" asked Sylva.

"If you wrap up warmly, including a hat,

Goldie," said Clara.

"I finally found a hat that makes me look adorable *and* keeps me warm," said Goldie. "Thank goodness."

"Let's go make snow fairies. Oh, but not you, Ginger," said Sylva. "The snow is too deep for a kitten. You stay here where it's warm." Ginger scampered over to the hearth rug and licked her fur by the fire.

"Mind you put your wings carefully on the wing table before you go out in the snow," said Clara. "I don't want them to get wet. You know it's not good for them." Clara remembered how wet her own wings had been during the Valentine's Games last year. "And frozen wings break right off!"

"It would have to get a lot colder before our wings broke off," said Sylva, laughing. "But we'll be careful!"

Sylva helped Goldie take off her wings, and

Goldie helped with Sylva's. "Are you coming, Rosy?" Goldie asked.

"I'm just bundling up Squeakie," said Rosy. "Your wings are too little to worry about, aren't they, Squeak?"

"*Humph*," said Squeak.

"*Humph?*" said Rosy, and she laughed. "I thought that was Goldie's favorite word."

"*Humph*," said Goldie. "That's not my favorite word. And besides, Squeak could be saying anything."

Rosy wasn't so sure that was true. She was the closest to Squeak, looking after her every day and watching her grow and change. She had never heard a word from Squeak that she could not understand.

"Come on," said Goldie. "Let's get outside before the winds kick up again."

The Fairy Bell sisters tromped out the front door of their fairy house—but they didn't get far before they all sank into the fresh snow. "It's all the way over my knees!" said Sylva. "Watch this!"

She stood up straight as a board, and then fell backward. "Keep your legs together!" shouted Goldie. "That's the way to make a perfect snow fairy."

"I already know that!" said Sylva. She spread her arms wide and fluttered them up and down. "Come on, Goldie. You make one too. And you too, Rosy. And Squeak! Tink will see them in our fairy garden when she flies overhead. One week exactly from today!"

The four Fairy Bell sisters made dozens of snow fairies on their white-blanketed lawn. "Look at Squeakie's!" said Rosy. She went over to where Squeak's snow fairy was. "How did you make those wings so big, Squeak, with those tiny arms you have? Your snow fairy looks as if she's going to get up and fly away."

"Sylva! Goldie! Is that you? Everything's so white I can barely see!"

"That's Poppy!" said Sylva. "And Avery is right behind her."

The Fairy Bell sisters were friends with everyone on the island, but Poppy and Avery were special. Poppy was Sylva's best friend—through thick and thin—and Avery was Goldie's. The two fairies landed with a soft thud just next to the Bell sisters' snow fairies. "These are beautiful," said Poppy. "Oh, and look at Squeakie's! Want to come with us? We're going to pick out our Christmas trees at the Christmas Tree Forest."

Avery brandished a rather fierce-looking hatchet. "I know how to chop wood from when I worked on the mainland. Caraway Cooke sent me this so I could chop down the biggest tree on the island."

"Well, keep it away from me!" said Goldie.

"The biggest tree on the island is as tall as a mountain," said Rosy. "But that will be good for cutting down the kind of trees we need."

"Come on, let's go!" said Sylva.

"Wait!"

Clara's voice rang out from the front door of the fairy house. "Rosy, Sylva, Goldie—we promised Tink we would let her do everything." Even as Clara said the words, she wanted to take them back. She loved choosing their Christmas tree each year and wanted to go with the other fairies to do just that. But she didn't want to disappoint Tinker Bell—not when Tink hadn't been home for Christmas in so long. "That includes choosing the tree."

Sylva's face fell. Goldie's mouth turned down at the corners. Even Rosy looked disappointed.

"That's right," said Sylva at last. "We promised Tink."

All five Fairy Bell sisters sighed a big sigh. It was Rosy who turned the moment bright again. "We didn't promise we wouldn't help our friends!" she said. "Come on, everybody, let's go pick out some Christmas trees! You too, Clara. Come on!"

Six

The Fairy Bell sisters and their friends flew up to Cathedral Pines, where Ginny and Genny, the Root sisters, planted trees every year for the Christmas Tree Forest. The trees above them were dizzying. "None of those, of course," said Poppy. "They're way too big. Ginny and Genny will have some just our size."

They flew over to a field of fairy-sized Christmas trees. "They'd all be perfect for us," whispered Sylva when she saw them.

"Tink will pick a gorgeous tree for you," said

Poppy. "The trees in Neverland are probably made of emeralds!"

"With Peter Pan's own arrowheads for decoration!" Sylva said, and the two friends grinned.

"Faith told me to pick whichever tree I like best for the schoolroom," said Avery. She started strolling through the rows of trees with Goldie at her side. "We have to make it look jolly for the Christmas Fair." Avery lived with her teacher, Faith Learned, above the fairy schoolhouse. Every year the Christmas Fair was held there. "I can't wait to do my Christmas shopping at the fair," Avery said. "On the mainland, the shops got so crowded—and I didn't have any way to pay for presents."

"That's so not fair!" said Sylva.

"I still can't believe that Queen Mab hands out sparkling stones—for free," said Avery. She had grown up on the mainland, and things were very different there.

"Of course she does," said Goldie, looking up at a tall blue spruce. "We get twelve each."

"Faith says they're called tourmaline," said Avery.

"Faith knows everything!" said Goldie. "Did she tell you they come in different colors? Wait till you see how polished they are, Avery. I hope

I get all green this year. Just like my eyes!"

"I like that we each get twelve stones," said Rosy as she ran her hand along the soft needles of a Scotch pine. "It's always more than enough to pay for what we'd like to buy—"

"I actually think *fifteen* stones would be better," said Goldie.

"—and anything we can't buy, we make ourselves," said Rosy.

"Tink did say we're not to buy any presents for one another," said Clara. She didn't like always being the one to remind her sisters about what Tink had said, but in fairness, she felt she had to.

"Because we'll get *so* many from her. I bet she'll raid Captain Hook's pirate ship for treasure!" said Sylva.

"What do you think your presents from Neverland will look like, Goldie?" asked Avery. "I can't even begin to imagine."

Goldie didn't answer right away. She was still a tiny bit peeved that Tink was going to bring their tree from Neverland. Goldie had very particular ideas about what a Christmas tree should look like. Last year she'd told Rosy, "It should be taller than a fairy, shorter than a troll, a perfect triangle from top to bottom, with soft green needles and a gorgeous sprucy smell to fill up the house." As that thought crossed her mind, she saw the absolutely most perfect Fraser fir tree right ahead of her. "Oh, this is the *most* beautiful tree on Sheepskerry!" she said. "It belongs in our fairy house."

"Except we're getting an emerald tree, from Neverland!" said Sylva.

"Sylva, sometimes you are so immature,"

said Goldie. "They don't have emerald trees in—"

"Ooh, that's gorgeous!" said a voice that came from just behind Goldie and Sylva. "We call that one for us!" And with that, Judy Jellicoe and her sister, Julia, swooped down into the forest next to Goldie's tree.

"Oh no!" said Goldie.

"Not to worry, Goldie," said Rosy. But before Rosy could even give Goldie a hug, dozens of Sheepskerry fairies filled the air and started to choose their Christmas trees.

"We call this one!" said Acorn Oak. "It's so pretty and we'll hang it with all our golden acorn caps."

"We call this one!" said the Shepherd sisters together.

On and on it went till the Christmas Tree Forest was just about empty. The Fairy Bell sisters watched the trees being cut down one by one. "We've been *robbed*," said Goldie.

"Well, not really," said Clara. "Sheepskerry Island is pretty full of trees."

"Not trees that have been specially grown for Christmas," said Goldie. "Just scraggly old leftovers. What if Tink forgets to bring us one?"

"What if she gets home and finds there's a tree already there?" asked Rosy, although to tell the truth, she had been thinking the same thing. "Tink's been away so long. Let's give her a chance to do something she wants to do for us."

"It's only another few days till Tink comes," said Sylva. "We can wait that long, I know we can." She gave her sisters a bright smile. "Let's at least get our ornaments out of the attic, in case she needs them to decorate," she said.

Sylva's enthusiasm was infectious. "Good idea," said Clara. "And how about a cup of hot peppermint tea to help us sort them all out?"

"Race you!" said Sylva. "And we'll get home

faster than any of the other fairies, since we don't have to lug home a big old Christmas tree!"

Sylva shot off with Goldie right behind her. Clara and Rosy—with Squeak squirming in her baby carrier—followed a little more slowly.

"Sylva's full of Christmas spirit," said Rosy. "I hope Tink makes it a wonderful Christmas for her."

"I hope so too," said Clara. But inside she added, *Mostly I hope she doesn't disappoint us all.*

Seven

"Ooh, it is so spooky up here!"

Sylva (who had won the flying race, of course) pulled down the trapdoor to the fairy house attic and peeked into the dark.

"We'll light a jellyfish lantern so we can see, but do be careful, Sylva," said Clara. "I meant to clear this out last spring, but I didn't manage to find the time. And don't let Ginger up here— we'll never find her if she decides to hide."

Goldie followed Clara up the steep steps to the attic. She didn't get to go up into the attic nearly as much as she liked to. She immediately flew over to the musty old costume trunk and opened its creaky lid. "This old-fashioned fairy dress is my favorite," said Goldie. "It suits me to a T."

"We're not here to try on clothes, Goldie," Clara said. "We're here to fetch the Christmas ornaments." She lifted her lantern, and the light shone on a dusty corner of the room. Sylva zipped up the stairs with Rosy right behind her, carrying Squeak.

"There they are!" said Rosy.

In a corner of the attic was a pile of boxes, all marked in different fairy handwriting: *Ornaments—special. Ornaments—old. Fairy lights—white. Fairy lights—colored. Sparkly things* (that was in Goldie's writing). *Wrapping paper. Ribbons. Boxes—used. Boxes—new.*

"Do you ever think we have too many things up here?" asked Clara.

"Never!" said Goldie and Sylva together.

"Where's the star, for the top of the tree?" asked Rosy. "Tink will want to put that on when she comes." She moved a pile of boxes. "It's not here with the other Christmas things. I think we put it somewhere so safe last year that we'll never be able to find it."

"Do you think she'll get here even earlier than she said? Tink, I mean," said Sylva. "Maybe she'll come tomorrow. There's only a week left till Christmas, you know."

"She said she'd be here early morning on Christmas Eve," said Goldie, wrapping herself in an old velvet cape.

"Don't get your heart set on seeing Tink early," said Clara.

"We'll see her when we see her," said Sylva. "I know."

"Help me carry down these boxes, Goldie," said Rosy. "I can't manage them all."

"I'll be right there," said Goldie. She was trying on the spun gold cloth that the Fairy Bell sisters wrapped around the base of their Christmas tree every year. "I think this could make a nice skirt for me."

"That's a tree skirt, not a fairy skirt," said Clara. "Tink brought it from Neverland when you were a baby, Goldie."

"I've always loved it," Goldie said. "It really should belong to me."

"It really should belong to all of us, which it does," said Clara. She held the gold cloth up to the light. "Tink said that this cloth came from Captain Hook's pirate chest. There's nothing else like it in the whole world."

"The other thing there's nothing like in the whole world is Tink's star," said Rosy. "We can't go down without it. Where can it be?"

If any of you are wondering why the fairies celebrate Christmas with so many familiar

customs—stars and trees, ornaments and presents—let me tell you why. Fairies and humans once mingled much more than they do now. As the ages passed, some traditions of the season were handed down from human people to the fairies, some from the fairies to human people. On Sheepskerry Island at least, it was hard to tell which was which.

"Doo!"

"Squeakie! How did you get there?" cried Rosy.

Squeak was all the way at the other side of the attic, where the fairies kept the wicker chairs they hoped to mend one day.

"You've found the star. And it *is* pretty, you're right!" said Goldie.

Squeak was holding up a box marked FRAGILE! *Tink's Star.*

"Good job, Squeak," said Rosy, taking it from her carefully. "I love this so much. Tink made it when I was just a little wee fairy like you."

Tinker Bell's star may be like the star you have on your own Christmas tree, but it may not be. "Stars aren't really pointy," she'd said when she made it, so many fairy years ago. "I've seen them up close. And shooting stars are the best of all." The Bell sisters loved their shooting star. It was so different from the ones on any other fairy trees. "That's why Tink is so . . . marvelous," said Sylva. "She thinks of things we would never think of."

"All I can think of right now is a nice hot bath," said Goldie. "This attic is so dusty."

"Don't use all the bubble bath," said Sylva.

"There would be a lot left if you hadn't tried to wash Ginger with it," said Goldie. "I'll use as much as I want."

"Oh, no you don't!" said Sylva as she chased

Goldie down the attic stairs.

"I think this may go on all night," said Rosy. "They're both so excited about Christmas."

"You know what, Rosy?" said Clara. "I'm beginning to get a good feeling about all this. Maybe Tink will even surprise us and arrive tomorrow morning."

"I hope she does, Clara," said Rosy. "Oh, I hope she does."

eight

But Tinker Bell did not arrive the next day. Nor the day after that. With only five days left till Christmas, every other fairy family was preparing for the big day. The Fairy Bell sisters could not help but feel left out.

And today was the Christmas Fair. Faith Learned's great-great-grandfairy had started this Sheepskerry Island tradition long ago. The fair was a grand celebration of all the fairies' talents. Every fairy brought along something lovely or useful or just plain fun to sell at the tables lined up in the schoolhouse. As far back as early autumn, the Fairy Bell sisters had worked on their contribution: pretty wind chimes, made of sea glass hung from driftwood with silver wires.

The morning of the fair, over a breakfast of oatmeal with currants and cinnamon, with steaming cocoa in their mugs, the sisters arrived at a decision.

"I know Tink doesn't want us to get one another presents for Christmas," said Clara carefully, "but I don't think she'd want us to go to the Christmas Fair just to look."

"I don't either!" said Goldie. "I absolutely *live* for the Christmas Fair!"

"What's your idea, Clara?" asked Rosy.

"Tink would want us to have the best Christmas Fair we could possibly have, so let's be each other's Secret Christmas Fairy."

"Secret Christmas Fairy?" asked Sylva. "How does that work?"

"Don't you know anything?" said Goldie.

"Goldie, please, I'll write all our names on different pieces of paper," said Clara, "like so."

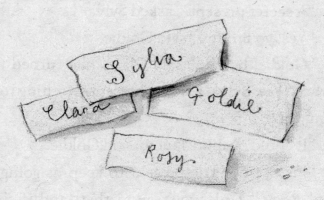

Clara wrote her sisters' names on separate pieces of paper in her best writing, except for Squeakie's, of course. "That's because we'll each get a little something for Squeakie," she said. She put the names into a pointy gnome's hat, left over from the Valentine's Games.

"Everybody choose one name," she said to her sisters.

"Then we each get a present for that sister?" asked Sylva.

"Exactly," said Clara.

"A secret present?" asked Sylva.

"Yes, you ninny," said Goldie.

"Goldie, be fair," said Clara. She turned to Sylva. "Yes, Sylva, a secret present. Nothing too fancy or big."

"It could be *quite* fancy," said Goldie.

"Just a tiny little present to keep us going," said Rosy. "Tink won't mind that, and if she does, I'll give her a piece of my mind." Clara and Rosy looked at each other. "Or not."

"Sylva," said Clara, "you draw the first name, since you're the youngest except for baby Squeak."

"Odeo!" said Squeak.

"Well, you are the baby of the family, Squeak, although someday I suppose you'll be grown."

Sylva dipped her hand into the gnome hat. *I*

hope I get Rosy, she thought. She opened up the scrap of paper and read the name.

"Don't say it aloud!" said Goldie.

Sylva looked again: *Goldie*. Her face only fell a little bit.

"I'm next!" said Goldie. "I hope I get my own name. Then I can get myself exactly what I want."

"If you get your own name, you have to throw it back," said Clara.

"*Humph*," said Goldie.

She scooped up a name and opened it quickly. *Sylva*, it said. "I guess I can live with that," said Goldie, "if I have to." Sylva could be so annoying, but Goldie did love her deep down.

"Your turn, Rosy," said Clara. Rosy put her hand into the gnome's hat. Rosy's paper said *Clara*. Rosy smiled.

"That leaves me," said Clara. And of course, as there was only one name left, Clara chose the paper that said *Rosy*. She could think of so many things Rosy would like.

Just then the clock on the mantel chimed twice.

"The Christmas Fair starts in half an hour!" said Goldie. "Let's go!"

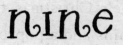

nine

The Fairy Bell sisters flew through the crisp winter wind to the fairy schoolhouse. They were so happy to glide into the toasty room, decorated so cheerily for Christmas. This particular Christmas, Avery and Faith had made the schoolhouse especially beautiful. They put away anything that made the place look like a schoolroom, scooping up all the books and maps and charts and hiding them in the cupboards. Then they pushed the desks into the center of the room and covered them with cloths of gold, silver, and deepest scarlet.

The rafters they strung with lights, the windows they brightened with candles, and in the corner was their Christmas tree—decorated with paper chains and a popcorn garland that the fairy school students had made.

"Can we help?" asked Rosy.

"I think we're just about finished," said Faith. "Avery made the wreath on the door—did you see it?"

"I should have known," said Goldie. "It has that Avery touch!"

At that moment, a great cloud of fairies flew through the door, bringing the cold in with them. Some of them had more items to add to the neatly organized tables. Some were swooping around to see if there were any bargains. All were full of the spirit of the season.

"Can I put my Christmas cookies here?"

"Is there a scarves and mittens table?"

"Where do you want us to put ornaments?"

"Ooh! Look at the jewelry display!"

Faith was so good at organizing and sorting that the fair was ready to begin. "But I think I'm forgetting something. What can it be?"

"You're forgetting Queen Mab!" Sylva said, laughing. "But here she is."

Queen Mab flew in through the schoolhouse doors. There was something more than magical about her, something serene and aglow from inside. All the fairies wanted to grow up to be just like Queen Mab.

"I love what she's wearing!" said Goldie.

Queen Mab was dressed in winter white— not a formal trailing gown but a much more comfortable outfit that would have been just right for ice-skating on Lupine Pond.

"She's really got style," Goldie added.

"My dear fairies," Queen Mab said in her lovely clear voice, and the crowd hushed. "Welcome, all, to the Christmas Fair." She smiled at all the fairies. "You have done a beautiful job making gifts that express your own skills." She looked around at the jams and jellies from the Jellicoe sisters; the shawls and wraps from the Cobweb sisters; the samplers and pillows from the Stitch sisters; the dried sea lavender from the Flower sisters; and the wind chimes from Clara, Rosy, Goldie, and Sylva.

Queen Mab flew high above them all. "Now Lady Courtney will give you each a dozen pieces of tourmaline from my own treasure chest, which you can use to buy gifts for family and friends. Lady Courtney, are you ready?"

Indeed she was. The fairies lined up, all of them in high spirits, laughing and chattering. It took just a few moments for Lady Courtney to distribute the beautiful polished stones to the fairies (everyone helped). Each group of twelve gemstones came in its own small purse.

"They're red this year!" Goldie cried when

Avery opened hers. "First time!"

"Shall we begin?" asked Queen Mab.

The fairies did not have to be asked twice. Up and down the aisles they flew, looking for the exact right gift for each fairy on their Christmas list.

ten

osy, with Squeak in her carrier, was the first to spot something perfect for her sister. "Look at that, Squeak!" Squeak just squirmed as Rosy flew over to the Cobweb sisters' table. There before her was the most beautiful shawl, worked in an intricate pattern of hearts and flowers. "That's some of my best work," said Lacey Cobweb.

"It's beautiful," said Rosy. "May I have it? For Clara?"

"I was hoping you'd spot this for Clara Bell," said Lacey. "I was thinking of her as I made it. It will cost you all twelve stones." She ran her hand over the lovely shawl. "But it's a fair price."

"It's worth twice that," said Rosy. She reached into her purse and found only three stones there. "That's funny," she said. "I thought we had twelve stones apiece."

"We do," said Lacey. "I'm going to buy a necklace for Blanche with my stones—and keep a little for myself so I can buy a silver charm bracelet, too."

"But where are the rest of *my* stones?" said Rosy. "Something must be wrong. I'll fly back to Lady Courtney to see what's going on."

Rosy didn't know it, but in another part of the Christmas Fair the same thing was happening.

"I'll take those green-and-silver shoelaces for Sylva," said Goldie as she and Avery looked over everything on the tables.

"She'll love them!" said Avery.

"I know," said Goldie. "They'll look so cute in her new sneakers."

"Plus, they only cost three stones," said Avery, "which leaves you . . ."

"I think it will leave me enough to buy that darling little skirt from the Stitch sisters. It's almost as pretty as the one in the attic."

"Even if that one is meant for a tree," said Avery. "Wait—you're buying something for yourself?"

"Of course I am!" said Goldie. "Sylva only likes little things anyway. And half the fun of the Christmas Fair is picking out things I've always wanted!" Goldie had expected to have lots of presents under a gorgeous Christmas tree by now, and since there were none, she thought it was only fair to treat herself to some little gift. *It's the least I deserve,* she thought, *waiting so long for Tink to come!*

"Come on, let's see how much you have."

Neither Avery nor Goldie was much good at doing math in their heads, but they could add and subtract very well when they had things they could hold in their hands. So they emptied out Goldie's purse to see how many stones would be left when they took three away.

Except there were only three stones in Goldie's purse.

Clara was having the same trouble. She had chosen some pretty coral earrings for Rosy, only to be turned down by the Seaside sisters when she hadn't enough stones to pay for them. "You must have spent them somewhere else, Clara," said Shellie Seaside. "Either that or you're trying to trick us into giving you a bargain."

"I'm not trying to trick you!" said Clara, her face hot. "Someone has tricked me!"

"Well, you can have the wire and the posts for three stones, and if you find coral on the beach, you can make the earrings yourself. But you may have to bargain with the mermaids for pieces as fine as this—and they're tougher than I am!" Shellie said.

Clara bought the wire and posts, more out of shame than anything else. She flew over to see Lady Courtney—only to find Rosy and Squeakie, Goldie, and Sylva already there.

"Oh dear me!" said Lady Courtney. "I had a feeling something like this was going to happen."

"We only get three measly stones apiece!" said Goldie. She was absolutely fuming. "I bet this is Tink's idea. She thought she'd have some fun with us."

"I knew those purses felt light when I gave them to you. But I had no idea Tink would pull such a trick on us all."

"Our whole Christmas is spoiled," said Goldie, and she stamped her foot. "All because of Tinker Bell. It's so unfair."

"Don't talk about Tink that way," said Sylva. "She's doing the best she can!" But Sylva herself was close to tears.

Queen Mab flew over to see what was upsetting the Fairy Bell sisters. "What is it, fairies?" she asked. "It's not at all like you to be sad at Christmastime."

Lady Courtney told her what Tink had done. "Which is why they got twelve stones between them," she concluded. "In fact, I think Tink has already sent the leftover stones to the poor fairies on the mainland. There was a note in the bottom of the treasure chest about it."

Now the Fairy Bell sisters felt really bad. They had so wanted the stones for themselves. But now Tink had sent the leftover stones to the poor fairies who needed them so much more than they did.

"Fairy Bells," said Queen Mab, "Tink is asking much of you. Possibly too much. I can fetch more tourmaline from my treasure chamber. Shall I?"

Clara looked at her sisters. All of them were so sad, especially poor Goldie, who adored shopping.

Sylva spoke at last. "Can we get through this . . . together?" she asked. "For Tink?"

Goldie blinked her eyes. Hard. "Maybe," she said in a small voice.

"I think we can," said Clara. "We only wanted to get a few small trinkets for one another to put under the tree—"

"Which we don't have," added Goldie.

"Three stones is still a lot," said Sylva. "Pretty much, anyway."

"You can't get much with three stones," said Goldie, "even if they are polished."

"Let's go back and see what we can find," said Clara. She wanted to be brave for her sisters, but she thought it was very hard on them, very hard indeed. "Come on, sisters. The spirit of the season isn't really about presents, anyway, is it?"

Goldie nodded, but she wasn't so sure.

"Let's sing a song to help us through," said Rosy.

"That's a good idea, Rosy. I think if you start a Christmas carol, all the fairies might join in," said Queen Mab. "It would be just the right thing for the Christmas Fair. And perhaps, to cheer up some fairy sisters who don't deserve to be sad."

It wasn't easy to sing with such heavy hearts. "What shall we sing?" asked Clara.

"Something festive," said Queen Mab. "I think it will cheer us all up."

The Fairy Bell sisters gathered close, and wrapping their arms around one another, they began to sing. They faltered a little at first, finding the note, but soon their voices joined together, strong and true:

Deck the fairy halls with holly,
Fa-la-la-la-la, la-la-la-la.
'Tis the season to be jolly,
Fa-la-la-la-la, la-la-la-la.
Spread our wings in fair apparel,
Fa-la-la, la-la-la, la-la-la.
Trill the ancient island carol,
Fa-la-la-la-la, la-la-la-la.

By the time they had sung the first verse,

they felt a bit better. The nice thing was that all the other fairies stopped their Christmas shopping and joined in on the next two verses. So, by the time they reached the last verse, there was a great chorus of voices making a joyful noise, and the Fairy Bell sisters' spirits lifted high:

Fa-la-la-la-la, la-la-la-la.

eleven

Everything would have gone pretty well after that, if it hadn't been for Sylva.

Sylva was following Goldie down the aisles of the Christmas Fair to try to get an idea of what her sister would really like for Christmas. Sylva could think of a hundred things for Goldie—she liked so much!—but with only three stones to use, she didn't want to waste a single one. Maybe she'd get three pairs of lacy socks from the Cobweb sisters, or a bracelet from the Gemstone sisters (if she could afford it), or—

Just then, Sylva saw Goldie holding up a green-and-orange bandanna.

"This would be perfect!" she said to Avery. They were both giggling. *Does Goldie really want that old bandanna for a Christmas present?* Sylva thought. Then she heard Goldie say, "It goes with everything. Too bad I don't have any

stones left to buy it for myself."

That was all Sylva needed. She swooped down to the table as soon as Goldie turned the corner and picked up the bandanna Goldie had just been holding.

"How much for this?" she asked Fern Stitch.

Fern checked her price list. "That's three stones," she said. "It used to be four, but since the fair is almost over . . ."

Sylva couldn't really believe she'd have to pay her only three stones for this not-very-nice bandanna, but . . . "This is what Goldie wants," she said. "And since Goldie's the only one I'm buying a present for—"

"The only one?" said Fern. "Why aren't you getting presents for your other sisters? Did you have a fight? That doesn't sound like you!"

"Of course we didn't have a fight. It's just that—well, Tinker Bell kind of changed the rules this Christmas."

At the sound of Tink's name, several fairies stopped to hear the news from Neverland.

"Tink changed the rules? What do you mean? Is she hoping to get here this year?"

"Hoping! She didn't say hoping," said Sylva. She didn't want the other fairies thinking that Tink would leave them hanging. "Tink says she's coming on the morning of Christmas Eve with our tree and our decorations and all our presents." By this time Sylva was grinning wide. She remembered how fantastic Christmas was going to be once Tink arrived. "She's been away so long, and now she's coming home."

"Oh, we can't wait to meet her!" said Fern. Many of the fairies on Sheepskerry had only heard of Tinker Bell in books. They gathered around now.

"You can all meet her," said Sylva. "You can all come over when she arrives. We'll have a huge surprise party for her!"

"Sylva, what are you talking about?" said Clara, who had flown by to see why the crowd was forming around her little sister. "We're not having—"

"Oh yes we are," said Sylva. "We're having a huge surprise party at four o'clock on Christmas Eve." She grinned at the fairies around her. "You're all invited! And Tink will be the guest of honor."

twelve

I'm sure I don't need to tell you that Sylva had acted a little too quickly. She got an earful from Clara about remembering *to check with her sisters* before she did something like that again. But Clara couldn't be upset with Sylva for long. Sylva was so excited about Tink's arrival that adding another ten or twelve fairies to the mix didn't seem such a bad idea.

As Rosy had said, "This is turning out to be such a topsy-turvy Christmas, I won't be surprised, no matter what happens."

So on the morning before Christmas, the

great room at the Fairy Bell sisters' house looked far from forlorn, even though there was no tree in the bay window and no wreath on the door. The presents the sisters had made for Tink and bought for one another at the Christmas Fair were wrapped in cheery paper and set out on the windowsill. Poppy came over that morning to help Sylva gather holly boughs to place in the rafters. "Tink won't mind that," said Poppy.

"Tink won't mind anything!" said Sylva. "She'll be so surprised when she gets here and finds so many fairy friends. She'll make the party such a magical event!"

"I'm sure it will be lovely whether Tink is here or not," said Poppy. "You sisters have done so much already."

"Oh, but Tink will put the magical touches on it all," said Sylva. "Without her it's just an ordinary tea party, but with her—it's completely special."

Sylva and Poppy cut as many holly branches as they could manage without getting too scratched by the pointy leaves. They flew back to the Fairy Bell sisters' fairy house with some difficulty. Not only were the boughs heavy in their arms, but the wind was blowing quite fiercely.

"That wind is really kicking up again," said Poppy. "I hope it won't blow Tink off course."

"Tink is so close to Sheepskerry by now that a little wind won't hurt," said Sylva, even as she and her best friend had to fight the gusts. "She'll be here in lots of time for the party. You wait and see."

Wait and see. Sylva wished she had never

said those words. Because waiting and waiting and waiting and *not* seeing was exactly what she and Poppy did that day. It wasn't so bad at breakfast time, as they knew Tinker Bell would not arrive in time for an early meal. But Tink had said the morning of Christmas Eve, and as the clock got closer and closer to noon, Sylva's heart sank.

"The other fairies will be coming for our Welcome Home Tink party so soon!" Sylva cried as the clock struck three. "She hasn't even arrived yet. We won't get to see her for more than a few minutes before everybody else arrives. It's not fair!"

"We might not get to see her at all at this rate," said Goldie. "I wouldn't be surprised if she just forgot—"

"Don't say such a thing, Goldie," said Rosy, who was almost never cross. But between all this waiting for Tinker Bell, and Squeakie's fussing, and Sylva's chatter, even Rosy's nerves were frayed.

"Yes, please, Goldie," said Clara. "Things are difficult enough today, now that Sylva has invited a dozen fairies to a magical tea."

"Now it's turned into *twenty* fairies, and I'll say what I want," said Goldie. "And it will probably turn out to be thirty fairies or more. All our fairy friends are bringing their fairy friends. We have about enough sandwiches and cakes for ten. Tink had better get here and get here fast." And she flew up to her bedroom and slammed the door.

"I'm not feeling very Christmassy," said Sylva.

"No lolo," said Squeak.

"That's about the first thing she's said that I've really understood this whole week," said Rosy. "What do you suppose is going on with her?"

"Can you please stop talking about Squeak

when I'm the one who needs love and care?" said Sylva. "No one is paying attention to me!" And she flew up to her room.

"We can't pay attention to you and take care of Squeak and make a party for twenty—"

"Thirty!" Sylva shouted.

"—thirty fairies at the same time!" said Clara. "Stop feeling sorry for yourself and get down here and help."

If you have a brother or sister or know someone who does, you'll understand exactly what was going on at the Fairy Bell sisters' house just then. Sylva was bitterly disappointed that Tink had not yet arrived. Goldie was still unhappy about not getting that skirt at the Christmas Fair. Rosy was preoccupied with Squeakie, and Clara was suddenly in charge of a party she did not want to give. In short, all the Fairy Bell sisters were upset and even a little bit angry, and they were pretty much taking it out on one another.

Ding-dong! the doorbell of the fairy house rang out.

"I'll get it!" said Poppy, glad to have something to do.

"If that is the Jellicoe sisters, I will just about have a fit," said Clara. "They always come early."

The front door opened, and in flew Judy and Julia Jellicoe. "We're here!" cried Judy.

"We were going to bring some jelly beans for the tea, but Sylva said not to bring a thing."

"Of course you're not to bring a thing," said Clara smoothly. "We have everything just about prepared. Why don't you take off your coats and hats while I get the party food from the kitchen?"

"You are ready for us, aren't you?" asked Julia. "I know we're a little bit on the early side, but I have to say it looks like—"

"It looks like we are absolutely ready," said Sylva, flying down from her room with her eyes only slightly red. Goldie and Rosy followed right behind her. When anyone else made them feel bad, the Fairy Bell sisters always rallied around one another, which was exactly what they were doing now.

"Welcome!" said Goldie.

"We're so pleased to have you," said Rosy.

"Bo-bo!" said Squeak.

The doorbell rang again (and again), and lots more fairies showed up.

"Where's Tinker Bell?"

"Is she visiting Queen Mab?"

"What did she bring you from Neverland?"

"Where's that tree with crystal branches?"

"I heard they were emerald."

Clara, Rosy, Goldie, and Sylva fended off the questions as best they could. To tell the truth, having so many fairies there, all needing another glass of blackberry punch or a new plate of pumpkin butter sandwiches, made the time

pass much faster than it had all week. "Tink must get here soon," said Iris Flower, checking the clock on the mantelpiece. "Christmas Eve will be over before you know it."

Indeed the clock was striking the hour of six, when the fairies usually would go home to be at their own fairy houses and prepare for Christmas morning. But they stayed just a little longer, in case Tink arrived at the last minute.

But she did not.

"We've waited long enough, I think," said Stemmy Stitch as the last chime of seven o'clock died away. "I'm so sorry Tink didn't manage to come to her own party."

"She's coming!" said Sylva fiercely. "She's just not here yet. You would have trouble flying from Neverland in this kind of weather, too!"

No one wanted to stay much longer after that outburst. Soon the last of the fairy guests drifted away until it was just the Fairy Bell sisters and their very best friends.

"I'm sure she'll be here very soon," said Avery as she hugged Goldie tight.

"I don't know if I even care anymore," said Goldie.

"Of course you do," said Avery. "And she *will* be here." She flew toward the door. "Faith and I will come over tomorrow morning to celebrate Christmas with you. We'll see you and your famous sister then."

"I hope so," said Goldie.

After Poppy and Sylva finally said their very long good-byes, there was nothing left but to clean up and go to bed, which is exactly what Sylva and Goldie did.

"I don't know if I can face these dishes," said Clara. "I thought all this would be done by magic. I thought for once that Tink would—" She dropped a plate on the floor, and it broke with a sharp crack.

"Oh, Clara. Don't say it," said Rosy, and she picked up the pieces. "Don't lose faith in Tinker Bell. She would be here if she could."

"Then why isn't she?" asked Clara. "Why hasn't she come, Rosy? Why did she have to ruin our Christmas just so she could be the star?"

"That's who she is, Clara. And we love so much about her—we have to love that too." Rosy put the dustpan and broom away in the cupboard. Then she hugged her sister tight. "Let's just leave the dishes for once and go to bed. Maybe Tink will come tomorrow, on Christmas Day."

"And if she doesn't?"

For a moment, Rosy was tempted to

say that Clara was right: If Tink didn't arrive, Christmas would be ruined. But then she thought of the way Goldie was trying so hard to make do with just a few presents, and how Squeakie was struggling to be understood, and how Sylva had been so brave when the guest of honor did not arrive at her own surprise party, and of course the way Clara held them all together.

"If she doesn't come," said Rosy, "we'll make it the best Christmas we can."

"You know what?" said Clara, taking off her apron. "Let's start right now."

thirteen

"Sylva! Goldie!" Clara's voice was brimming with mischief. "Come down here right now."

"What is it, Clara?" asked Rosy.

"You'll see," said Clara.

Sylva and Goldie came down to the great room in their pajamas, while Squeakie slept soundly in her crib.

"Tink's not here, is she?" asked Sylva.

"Nope, not yet, and let's stop talking about when she'll come and what she'll bring. Let's celebrate being here together with one another.

If she arrives tomorrow, it will be lovely to see her. And if she doesn't—"

"If she *doesn't*?" said Sylva, her face falling.

"If she doesn't," said Clara firmly, "then we will send her our love and promise to come visit her in Neverland next year."

"We'd go to *Neverland*?" said Rosy.

"Why not?" said Goldie. "I wonder what exactly those Lost Boys are like."

"We'll go together, and see Tink next year, and bring Christmas to her," Clara said. "By next year I should have just about enough magic to get us there."

"Maybe Queen Mab will send us in her Royal Balloon!" said Sylva.

"You're right!" said Clara. "But why are we talking about next Christmas, when it's practically Christmas right now? We've got some presents to open!"

"Are you sure Tink won't mind?" asked Sylva.

"I'm very sure," said Clara. "Tink may get distracted and not do everything quite as she hopes to, but I know for a fact she would not want Christmas to be spoiled for us."

"Let's take a vote. All in favor of opening our presents right now, say aye!" Goldie declared.

"Aye!" said Rosy, Clara, and Sylva.

"All opposed, say nay!" said Goldie.

No one said nay, but Ginger said *Mow*, which made them all laugh.

"Then let's begin!" said Goldie.

They gathered their small pile of presents around them. In the light of the fire, it looked like a treasure.

"Let's go oldest to youngest this time," said Sylva. "I want to save mine for last."

Rosy handed Clara a package. "I was your Secret Christmas Fairy," she said. "I wrapped it in a tea towel, see?"

"Ooh, I love it, Rosy," said Clara.

"It's part of your present," said Rosy.

Clara secretly hoped that Rosy's entire Secret Christmas Fairy gift was not going to be about drying dishes, but she didn't say anything in case that's what Rosy had chosen for her.

When she opened up the tea towel, she could hardly believe her eyes.

"It's the shawl I wanted, from the Cobweb sisters! Oh, Rosy, how did you do that? It cost far more than three polished stones."

"The Cobwebs were kind," said Rosy. "They gave me the pattern, and I crocheted it myself. Don't look too closely!" She did not say that she had been up hours every night since the Christmas Fair finishing the shawl for Clara. Her reward was the happiness on Clara's face.

Clara wrapped the shawl around her slender shoulders. Its warm turquoises and corals set off her dark skin and dark eyes. "You should wear that at the next Valentine's Games!" said

Sylva. "Rowan won't be able to take his eyes off you!"

"He already has trouble doing that," said Goldie.

Clara's cheeks flushed. "How about you, Rosy? Here's one for you! I was your Secret Christmas Fairy."

Rosy looked at the tiny package in front of her.

"Three stones is not a whole lot to work with," said Clara.

"Oh, I love tiny packages, you know that, Clara," said Rosy. "I just like to take my time." She gave her big sister a hug, then unwrapped the little box to find sweet shell earrings inside.

"This was just what I'd hoped for," she said. "How did you know?"

"I wanted to get you coral, but the mermaids wouldn't cooperate," said Clara. "I had to make these myself, so if they're a little clumsy, you'll know why."

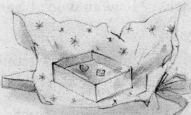

"I think they're lovely," said Rosy, slipping the earrings on. "I wouldn't have wanted coral, anyway." That was only a little bit of a fib. "These suit me perfectly." She gave Clara another hug. Her big sister loved her so much.

"I know I said I'd go last, but can I go next?" asked Sylva. "I can't wait anymore!"

"Of course you can go next," said Clara. A tree branch rattled against the windowpane. "Just listen to that wind."

"I know. It's really howling," said Rosy. "It almost sounds like a cat or a bird or—"

"No one would be out on a night like this, Rosy," said Clara.

Goldie handed Sylva her present. "It's not

much," said Goldie. "But I hope you like it."

"This paper is amazing!" said Sylva. "It's practically a present itself."

"I designed it myself," said Goldie. "It's part of my line."

"Let's see what's inside," said Sylva. She peeked into the package. "Oh! It's laces for my fairy running shoes!" she said. "I love these, I love these," she sang. "They are perfect colors and just what I wanted. I'm going to put them on right now!" She flew over to the mudroom and fetched her running shoes. The new laces were tied up in no time. "These look great!" said Sylva, admiring them on her feet. "Thank you, Goldie. Merry Christmas!"

Goldie began to feel a little bit better about the presents her sisters were getting for Christmas. Maybe Sylva, too, had picked out the perfect present at the Christmas Fair. *There were so many things that could have been perfect for me,* she thought.

"Open yours, Goldie!" said Sylva. "Open yours!"

Goldie tore through the wrapping paper, which had been haphazardly put on by Sylva. "It's just what you wanted, isn't it? You said, you said!"

Goldie's face fell. It was the secondhand green-and-orange bandanna. The one she had been making fun of with Avery at the Stitch sisters' stand.

"You really thought I'd like this?" said Goldie. She was close to tears.

"At first I didn't really believe that you and Avery would even notice such a thing, but then you talked about it so much I knew you really meant it," Sylva said. She was so happy with her gift that she didn't notice Goldie's eyes were glistening. "You're so good at accessorizing, Goldie. I know you'll make this look fabulous somehow."

She gave Goldie a big hug. "I'm so happy I could get you exactly what you wanted for Christmas!"

Goldie gave Sylva a hug back. "Merry Christmas, Sylva," said Goldie softly.

Clara saw Goldie brush away a tear, and her heart melted. She whispered something to Sylva, who whispered to Rosy, who nodded.

"What is it?" asked Goldie.

"Wait there just one minute . . . ," said Sylva. She flew over to the stack of Christmas ornaments laid out for Tinker Bell and pulled something out from the bottom. "It's the *second* part of your present," said Sylva, her face shining. "We're giving you the Christmas tree skirt, Goldie!"

"But that belongs to everyone," said Goldie.

"Not now!" said Clara.

"Try it on, Goldie," said Rosy.

"Really?" asked Goldie.

"Yes, please!" said her sisters.

Goldie whipped the elegant Christmas tree skirt around her waist. She tied a bow in the back. The golden fabric glowed in the firelight and caught the light in Goldie's long hair.

The sisters had seen that tree skirt around the Christmas tree for years, but on Goldie it took on new life.

"You're gorgeous!" said Clara simply.

"Oh, thank you!" cried Goldie. "Thank you, all!"

The four Fairy Bell sisters sat in the glow of the dying fire. There was no tree, just a few gifts, no Christmas feast, and Tink had not come. And yet, this was the best Christmas they had ever had.

"Shall we get ready for bed now?" asked Clara. "Tomorrow's Christmas Day. We'll visit everyone in the fairy village—"

"And we'll feast at Queen Mab's palace," said Sylva.

"And we'll help Squeakie open all her presents when she wakes up bright and early. Won't we, Squeak?"

The sisters got up to look into Squeak's fairy crib. "She must have been awfully tired. I haven't heard a peep from her for ages," said Clara.

"Are you asleep, Squeak?" asked Rosy softly as she leaned over the crib. "Or are you—"

Rosy let out a gasp.

"Oh no! Oh no!" she cried. "Squeak's gone!"

fourteen

Clara, Rosy, Goldie, and Sylva looked all over their fairy house for baby Squeak. They did not find her. Anywhere.

"She must be hiding somewhere to play a trick on us. Squeak, come on now. It's not funny anymore. Where are you?"

"She's not here, Clara," said Rosy. "I can feel it. She's gone. I don't know how or what has happened, but she has gone."

"If she's gone, she can't have gone far. She's too tiny. She must have crawled under one of the beds. Sylva, go check again."

Sylva flew upstairs to the bedrooms, but Rosy felt in her fairy wingtips that something was not right. Squeak had been acting so strangely for the past few weeks. "I should have known something was the matter with her. What did she want me to know?" Rosy's wings kept quivering. "She was trying to tell me something. But what?"

Some instinct made Rosy go to the back door of the fairy house. "Clara, look. It's open a crack. She went outside for some reason. Oh, it's freezing out there." Clara took one step out the door and knew Rosy was right. It was freezing outside. In fact, the temperature had been dropping all evening. "We have to find her!" said Clara. She, Rosy, Goldie, and Sylva gathered what hats and coats they could find and rushed out the back door, Goldie with a lantern in hand.

"Follow her tracks in the snow!" said Sylva.

"Look! I see them! We'll find her in no time now!"

None of the sisters wanted to say what they were all thinking. It was bitterly cold out on Sheepskerry Island, with the wind whipping and the snow swirling. A little baby fairy could not get far.

"Here are more of her little footprints!" said Sylva. "They're heading straight out our front garden to—"

Sylva stopped short. The tracks disappeared. "There's nothing else here," she said. "It's as if . . . she disappeared."

Goldie, Clara, and Rosy rushed over to where Sylva stood. "Those are her footprints," said Goldie. "But where did she go from here?"

"Did someone come fetch her?" asked Clara.

"No, they would have brought her back home," said Rosy.

"Did she fall and hurt herself?" Sylva asked.

"There's no sign of that," said Clara.

"Then where oh where can she be?" Rosy cried.

Sylva leaned down and looked carefully at the footprints in the snow. "Look, everybody," she said. "They get closer together right here."

"And then . . . nothing," said Rosy. She was on the verge of panicky tears. "It's almost like someone snatched her away."

"Or . . . ," said Clara, "as if she flew."

fifteen

Once the Fairy Bell sisters realized that baby Squeak might be able to fly, they were filled with wonder and relief—and even more panic. Where could she have gone? And why?

"Let's calm down and use our heads," said Clara.

"We can look for flying tracks," said Sylva. "She can't be completely sure of herself yet. She must have left tracks in the trees."

Sure enough, Sylva was right. The sisters looked up at the trees above Squeak's last footprints. "Look!" Goldie said. "Heading toward the east shore! The branches are broken."

"Goldie's right," said Clara. "She must have started this way. And, oh look, some more footprints!"

Bit by bit, the Fairy Bell sisters followed Squeakie's clumsy trail through the Fairy Village, around Sunrise Hill, in the direction of the Fairy Library.

"I can't believe how far she flew," said Rosy. "Where could she be going?"

"I think she must be looking for Tink," said Clara.

"I don't think that's it," said Rosy. "She was trying to tell me something, but I didn't listen. Oh, Squeakie—I am so sorry!"

"We all could have listened better," said Goldie. She hated to see Rosy upset. "But we can't dwell on that. We need to find her. Oh, look!" Her eyes lit up. "She landed here. You can tell by the snow!"

Indeed, there was a big dent in the snow, just beyond the Fairy Library near the east shore. "Squeakie! Are you here? Where did you go?"

Then they heard something. "What was that?" said Clara. "A loon?"

"There won't be any loons out on such a cold night," said Sylva. She drew her jacket around her.

The strange cry came again. "A cat?" asked Goldie.

"Ginger is safe at home," said Sylva. "And Poppy wouldn't let Lucky out on a night like this."

The sisters listened again. "That's not Squeak's voice, I know that much," said Rosy. "It's that cry I heard before—when we were opening our presents. It sounds more like—"

"Look—over there on Heart Island! Can you

see something?"

Clara, Rosy, Goldie, and Sylva strained their eyes as they looked over onto the little island off Sheepskerry's east shore. "I think I see her!" cried Rosy. "I think she's there on Heart Island."

"What is she doing there?" said Goldie. "Did she run away from home?"

"Squeak would never run away from home," said Clara. "Something must be up. Come on, sisters, we have no time to lose." Clara could feel her wings starting to freeze. And if her wings were freezing, Squeak's must be freezing too.

Sixteen

Rosy knew they were lucky—the wind was out of the west and blew them over to Heart Island with no wear and tear on their wings, which were stiff from the cold. *How we'll get back is anyone's guess*, Rosy thought. "Oh, why didn't we stop to ask for Queen Mab's help?"

"We didn't have time," Clara replied. "We did the right thing." Clara didn't even want to think about what might have happened if they hadn't acted as quickly as they had.

"She's right in the middle of the island," said

Sylva. "I guess it must be a loon—"

"It's a cat, I think," said Goldie.

"—whatever it is, the sound is coming from the middle of the island. Not much farther now."

In the very middle of Heart Island, there's a rock that looks like a heart itself. At the top of the rock, there's a little cleft, which makes a shelter. That's where the noise was coming from. And that's where the Fairy Bell sisters found Squeakie Bell.

"Oh, Squeak! You're all right!" cried Clara. "You're all right!"

All the Fairy Bell sisters rushed over to give her a hug. And I don't mind telling you: Many tears were shed.

"Why did you leave us?"

"How did you fly so far?"

Then the little cry came again. "What's making that noise, Squeak?" They looked carefully. Squeak was sitting in the shelter of the rock, and

nestled in her lap was something even smaller than she was.

"What have you got there, Squeak?" asked Clara.

Rosy was the first to realize. "Oh my!" she said. "The question is not *what* have you got there. It's *who* have you got there."

And Squeak said, "Baby."

Seventeen

"Squeak! You said a word!" said Goldie.
"You said 'baby'!"

"A real word," said Clara. "Oh, Squeakie, we are so proud of you!"

"Not to mention you rescued a new baby fairy!" said Sylva.

It didn't take long for the Fairy Bell sisters to figure out what had happened. (Nor you, I'm sure!) Squeak had been out of sorts because her wings ached from learning to fly.

Her sisters hadn't thought it possible that she'd be flying so early—most fairies don't learn till they're five fairy years old, and Squeakie was barely two. Little fairies have a knack for understanding or hearing one another, so it was no wonder that Squeak heard this little fairy's cries despite the wind and the distance.

Most fairy babies are not born in the winter, because it's so cold that human children often are busier keeping themselves warm than laughing. (Fairies are born when a human child laughs for the first time, as some of you already know.) And most fairy babies land in a safe place with their sisters gathered around them . . . but this one did not.

"Thank goodness she wasn't harmed!" said Clara.

"You saved her life, Squeak," said Rosy.

Now the question was, what to do next?

"Baby," said Squeak again.

"We see, Squeak!" said Sylva. "We see it's a new baby." She turned to her sisters. "Shouldn't we get her home?"

The five Fairy Bell sisters looked into the night. The temperature had continued to drop. And the wind was against them. "We flew out here, but we may not be able to fly back!" said Goldie. "With this cold, our wings might snap right off."

"We can walk back to the island if it's low tide," said Sylva. But one glance at the rocks showed them that the tide had flooded in while the fairies were looking for Squeak. "We can't walk. And we can't fly. And if this baby does not get in out of the snow before long, she might—"

"Don't even say it!" said Rosy. "We have got to get her back to our fairy house. And Squeakie, too. She's freezing!"

The Fairy Bell sisters looked over at Squeakie and the tiny fairy baby. The temperature was way below freezing. The wind was bitter. But since there was no proper shelter on Heart Island, the only way to safety was to fly home. Fast.

"Squeak's teeth are chattering. Oh, Squeakie, what possessed you to come out in this tiny little fairy dress? And no coat or hat?"

"Baby," said Squeak.

"I know!" said Rosy. "You wanted to take care of the baby. And that was just the right thing to do. But now how will we take care of you?"

Clara pulled off the shawl Rosy had just given her for Christmas. "Let's wrap you up, Squeak, and the baby too." Clara tried to wrap the two little fairies in her new shawl, but the baby was too squirmy to keep it on, so it kept falling off Squeakie, too.

"Tear it in half, Clara," said Rosy. "It's the only way to keep them both warm!"

"But you worked so hard on it!" said Clara.

"It doesn't matter now," said Rosy. "Those little ones need it more than any of us. I'll make you another, Clara, but not in time for Christmas!"

Without wasting another moment, Clara tore Rosy's carefully crocheted stitches on a rock. Then she ripped the beautiful shawl in two. "I'm sorry, Rosy!" she said. But Rosy was busy wrapping up the baby in one half of the shawl as Clara wrapped Squeak in the other.

"Their teeth aren't chattering anymore," said Sylva. "Hold them close! I think they're going to be okay!"

"But how will we get off Heart Island and back to Sheepskerry?" said Clara. She tentatively stretched out a wing. The wind had died down, and the temperature seemed to be

holding steady. "I think we have a few minutes to get across without snapping our wings off," she called. "But I don't know how we'll be able to fly into the wind and hold these little ones at the same time!"

Sylva thought of it first. "If we can make some kind of baby carriers, you could keep the baby safe, Rosy. And Clara can hold Squeakie the same way. But we have to do it fast." She squinted at the horizon. "It looks like there might be a snowstorm on the way."

"Here!" said Goldie. "Use my skirt!"

"We can't do that to you, Goldie!" cried Clara.

"These babies need it. We all need it. So let's use it, please!"

"I know!" said Sylva. And she whipped the green-and-silver shoelaces out of her new shoes. "We can use these to tie up the baby carriers. It's got to work somehow."

"But your feet will freeze without your sneakers!"

"I'll hang on to these sneakers, don't worry about that."

In a moment, Goldie had torn her skirt into strips and swaddled the baby on Rosy's chest. "Oh, this won't stay!" cried Goldie. "The laces are too slippery to hold a knot like this!"

Without a word, Rosy took off one of her

treasured earrings, unbent the wire, and twisted them onto her baby carrier. "There," said Rosy. "Not as good as a safety pin, but it will hold." She did the same for Clara and Squeakie.

"Do you really think we can get across?" asked Sylva. It wasn't like her to be afraid, but the storm was fearsome, the sky dark, the winds fierce, the water beating against the rocks. "If we get weak or tired we may—"

"If we're weak or tired, we will pull each other through!" said Goldie.

"We can do this, sisters," said Clara.

"We *must* do this to save ourselves," said Rosy. "And to save the . . ."

She waited for Squeak to say "baby." But Squeak was too weak to say a word.

eighteen

Out into the fearsome wind they flew. I can barely imagine how they did it. There hadn't been quite enough food at the party, so none of them had had much to eat since their breakfast hours and hours ago. Halfway between Heart Island and Sheepskerry they were blown back out to sea, which meant their journey was even longer than it should have been. They looked in vain for help from seals or seabirds, but no other creature was foolish enough to venture out in this kind of cruel winter wind.

"Hold on, Squeak," said Clara. "Hold on and we will get you warm and safe again."

Rosy could tell that the baby fairy was still all right, thanks to the baby carrier Goldie had made. Still, she was squirming and fussing. "Be still, little one," said Rosy. "I promise we will keep you safe from harm." But even as she said the words, she didn't know if she could keep her promise.

"We have to give her a name!" called Sylva as she flew. "Oops, there goes my sneaker!"

"Not now, Sylva," said Clara.

"Yes, now! I've got to take my mind off this wind somehow."

"Okay!" called Rosy over the wind. "She was born one day before Christmas, so something Christmassy."

"Holly?" called Sylva.

"Star?" cried Goldie.

"Poinsettia?" asked Rosy.

"Definitely not Poinsettia," said Goldie.

"How about Noel?" said Clara. And even with the wind howling in her ears, Clara could hear the baby laugh. "Noel it is, then," she said in a whisper.

"Land!" cried Sylva. "Sheepskerry Island, twenty yards away."

Through the darkness, the Fairy Bell sisters could just see the outline of the tall spruce trees on Sheepskerry's shore. "There's White Rose Cottage!" cried Rosy. She had never been so happy to see a place in her life.

"Shall we stop there and rest?" asked Goldie. "I think I can go on, but you two must be exhausted, carrying those little ones."

"Let's press on!" cried Clara. "I can do it now. Can you, Rosy?"

"I can!" cried Rosy.

The Fairy Bell sisters put on a final burst of speed and in a trice were on the path back to their fairy house.

"Oh no, Clara!" cried Rosy. "Our house! What's the matter?"

There was a strange glowing coming from the Bell sisters' fairy house. *It couldn't be on fire, could it?* thought Clara, her heart racing. *Not after all we've been through.*

"Hurry!"

Though their wings were exhausted with the effort, and their hands and faces raw with the cold, the sisters pushed on to their house.

"If our house is gone, we'll manage somehow," said Rosy. "The Flower sisters will take us in, or Queen Mab."

"But all our pretty things—they can't all be burned to the ground, can they?"

As the sisters flew closer and closer to their fairy house, the glow only got brighter. But one by one they began to think that perhaps it wasn't fire after all.

"I don't think our house is on fire," said Rosy. "There's no smoke."

"And no flames," said Clara. "But feel how warm it is!"

They landed on the lawn of their fairy house. The house was not on fire. It was lit with a brilliant light from inside. The light was so strong and clear that Squeakie's eyes opened for a moment. "Ahhma," she said.

"Open the door, Clara," said Sylva. "See if it really is magic."

Clara tentatively put her hand on the doorknob. She turned it gently and then flung it wide.

The great room was dazzling. Where there had been an empty space, now there was a giant Christmas tree hung with every imaginable decoration, and Tink's star on top. Where there had been a few torn pieces of wrapping paper on the floor, now there was an enormous pile of presents, teetering almost to the ceiling. There was a glorious feast on the table, and a wreath was hung above the mantelpiece. The smell of cinnamon and brown sugar was in the air.

Steaming mugs of hot chocolate stood on the large oak table. Even the air of the great room was filled with the sound of delicate bells.

And in the middle of it stood someone they all knew.

"Oh, Tink! Tink!" cried the Fairy Bell sisters all at once. "You've come home. You've come home at last."

nineteen

Oh, what a feast they had! What a glorious reunion for all six Fairy Bells! So much love was there in the fairy sisters' house, Rosy thought it might burst from all the happiness inside it.

The clock had long since chimed midnight, and the sisters could not wait till the morning to celebrate. So they dug into their feast and opened gift after gift and sang till their voices wore out.

Later Clara thought there must have been magic involved, because Christmas night seemed to last forever. They finally dropped into their beds, exhausted, asleep before their heads sank into their pillows. Tink took care of the tiny new baby fairy and tenderly tucked in Squeakie when she'd stopped flying around. "We can't call her baby Squeakie anymore," said Clara.

"Not when there's a new baby in the house," said Sylva.

None of the Fairy Bell sisters saw the dawn, but it broke bright and clear. The glow from the Bell sisters' house could be seen even in the daylight, and soon all the fairies of Sheepskerry came to visit Tinker Bell and her sisters. Tink led them in a merry procession to Queen Mab's palace, where they gathered for a festival of song and story. Tink told them tales of Neverland that would fill a book longer than this one. Finally the sun set over Sheepskerry Bay, and Christmas Day was over.

Tink and her sisters said one last farewell.

"Are you really going so soon?" asked Sylva.

"Come back again, Tink!" said Clara.

Tinker Bell kissed each of her sisters (and baby Noel) in turn. Then she raised her wings and flew away.

Where Tink had stood, a trail of sparkles swirled in her place. "There's one last Christmas surprise for you," they chimed. "Can't wait till you discover it!"

As Clara turned back into the fairy house, she thought she would be lonely without her big sister, Tinker Bell, there. But the house was so full of love and magic that Tink's glow wrapped around them all and filled them with even more joy.

"I suppose we should get ready for bed," said Clara. "It's been such a long day."

"I'm so tired I could absolutely drop," said Goldie, admiring her new skirt of spun gold. Tinker Bell had magicked her a new one, from

Neverland. "I wonder if I can wear this to bed."

"I'd wear these sneakers to bed if I could," said Sylva. "They'll make me go even faster than the ones I lost—or the one I lost, I should say." Tink had made new sneakers appear by magic for her little sister.

Rosy took the sweet coral earrings off her ears and laid them carefully on her dresser. "Tink knows just what I like," she said as she tucked Squeakie in.

"Baby?" said Squeakie.

"Clara's taking care of our new baby sister, Squeak," said Rosy. "Don't you worry." Rosy called to her older sister as she started work on a new shawl for her, "Have you found the stack of clothes Tink laid out for her?"

"I have!" called Clara. "What an odd assortment she chose, though," she said to herself. "None of Goldie's old things, and hardly any of Rosy's or mine. They're all bits and pieces from our old play chest. What was Tink thinking?"

Sylva, Goldie, Rosy, and Squeak had just laid their heads on their pillows when a shriek came from Clara downstairs, followed by a great peal of laughter from baby Noel.

"Clara! What is it? Is everything all right?"

"Oh my golly," said Clara. "I think I've found that last surprise Tink said we'd discover."

That was enough to get everyone out of bed. The sisters flew down the stairs, Squeak leading the way.

"What is it?" asked Goldie. "What's the surprise? More presents?" Even Goldie didn't think she could take any more.

"Another baby?" Rosy was only half-kidding.

"Another kitten?" asked Sylva. "Or a puppy?"

"I've got news for you," said Clara as she came back with baby Noel freshly cleaned and changed in her arms. "Our new fairy sister . . . is a boy."

twenty

When they'd stopped exclaiming and wondering and laughing, the Fairy Bell sisters headed to bed, with Squeak sleeping on a spare mattress on Sylva's floor and their new baby *brother* fairy taking Squeak's place in the crib in the great room.

"We'll love this little fairy no matter what," said Rosy.

"Boy oh boy, is everyone going to be very surprised," said Sylva.

"Boy oh boy is right!" said Goldie.

"We just need to give him love and care and a happy home," said Clara.

"That's what all little ones need," said Rosy. "That's the recipe for a happy—"

"Baby," said Squeak.

And they went to bed that Christmas night, dreaming of Tinker Bell and Christmas magic and new fairy babies, and all the adventures that lay ahead of them.

fairy secrets

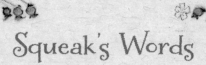

Squeak's Words

O-bee!: Not me!

Ahhma!: Oh my!

Doo!: Pretty!

Odeo!: Oh dear!

No lolo: Don't be sad.

Bo-bo!: Welcome!

How to Make
Fairy Bell Holiday Punch

The secret of a perfect party? Perfect punch! Here's what the Fairy Bell sisters serve when they're expecting a big crowd. (Ask a grown-up to help.)

1 quart fairy apple cider made from Sheepskerry apples*

1 cup cranberry juice from fairy cranberry bogs*

2 cups chilled fairy ginger ale from the shops on the mainland*

A little lemon juice (fairy or non-fairy— your choice)

Combine the cider, the cranberry juice, and the lemon juice in a large bowl. Chill on the back porch of your fairy house or in a refrigerator. When the mixture is nice and cold, add the ginger ale, stir, and serve to fairy friends.

Try adding some orange or apple slices to make your punch especially pretty.

* If fairy cider, fairy cranberry juice, and fairy ginger ale are not available, a grown-up can buy these ingredients at your local grocery store.

Deck the Fairy Halls

Deck the fai- ry halls with hol- ly, Fa- la- la- la- la- la- la- la- la.

'Tis the sea- son to be jol- ly, Fa- la- la- la- la- la- la- la- la.

Spread our wings in fair ap- par- el, Fa- la- la- la- la- la- la- la- la.

Trill the an- cient is- land car- ol, Fa- la- la- la- la- la- la- la- la.

Fast away the old year passes,
Fa-la-la-la-la, la-la-la-la.
Hail the new, ye fairy lasses,
Fa-la-la-la-la, la-la-la-la.
Sing we joyous, all together,
Fa-la-la, la-la-la, la-la-la.
Heedless of the wind and weather,
Fa-la-la-la-la, la-la-la-la.

Meet the
Fairy Bell Sisters!